SCHOLASTIC INC.

NEW YORK   TORONTO   LONDON   AUCKLAND
SYDNEY   MEXICO CITY   NEW DELHI   HONG KONG

No part of this publication may be reproduced, stored in a retrieval system, or transmitted in any form or by any means, electronic, mechanical, photocopying, recording, or otherwise, without written permission of the publisher. For information regarding permission, write to Scholastic Inc., Attention: Permissions Department, 557 Broadway, New York, NY 10012.

ISBN 978-0-545-33136-4

Copyright © 2010 by James Proimos.
All rights reserved. Published by Scholastic Inc. SCHOLASTIC and associated logos are trademarks and/or registered trademarks of Scholastic Inc.

12 11 10 9 8 7 6 5 4 3 2 1   11 12 13 14 15 16/0

Printed in the U.S.A.   40

First Scholastic paperback printing, January 2011

The text was hand-lettered by Lerch.
The illustrations were done in ink and Photoshop.
Book design by Becky Terhune

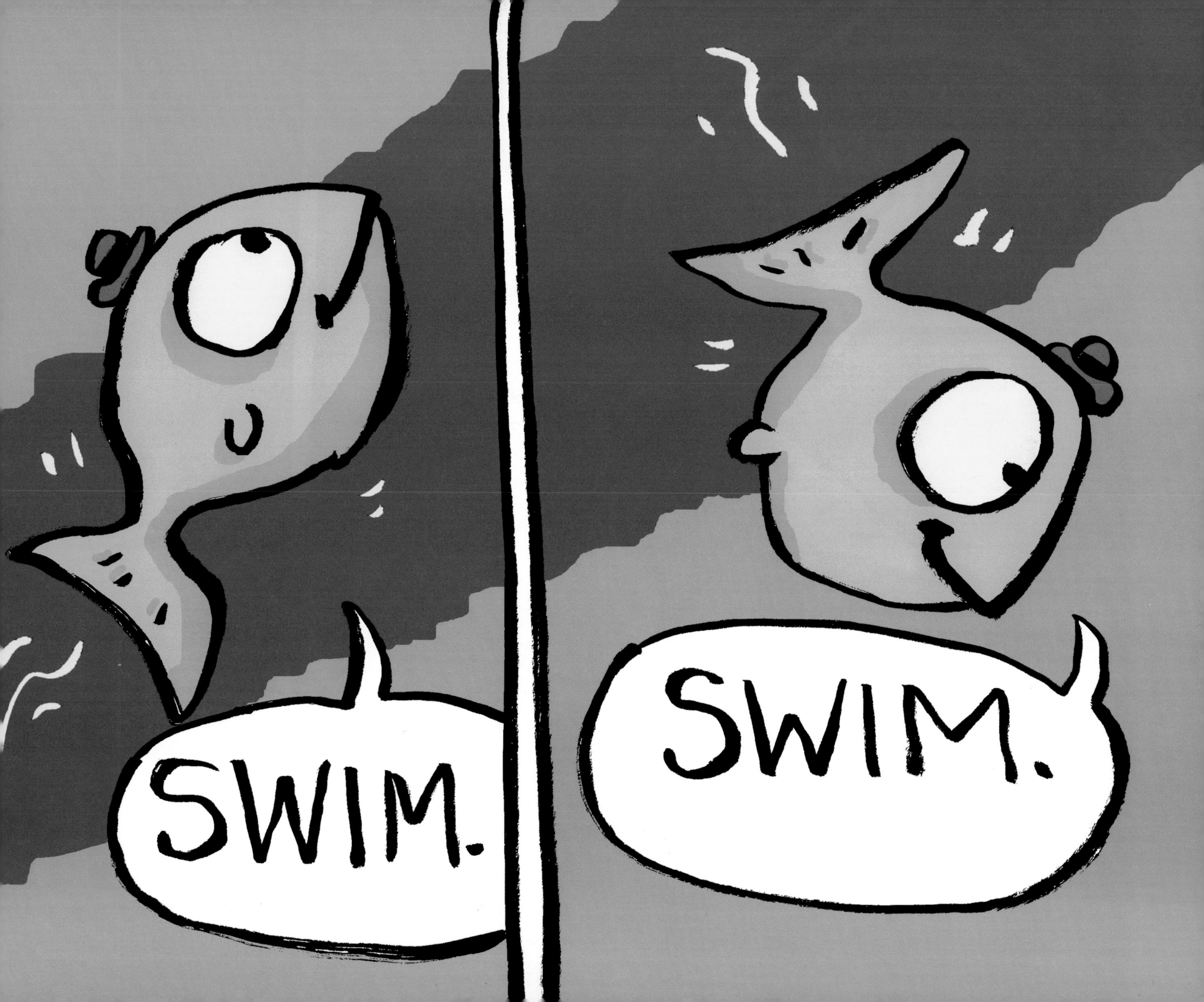
SWIM.
SWIM.

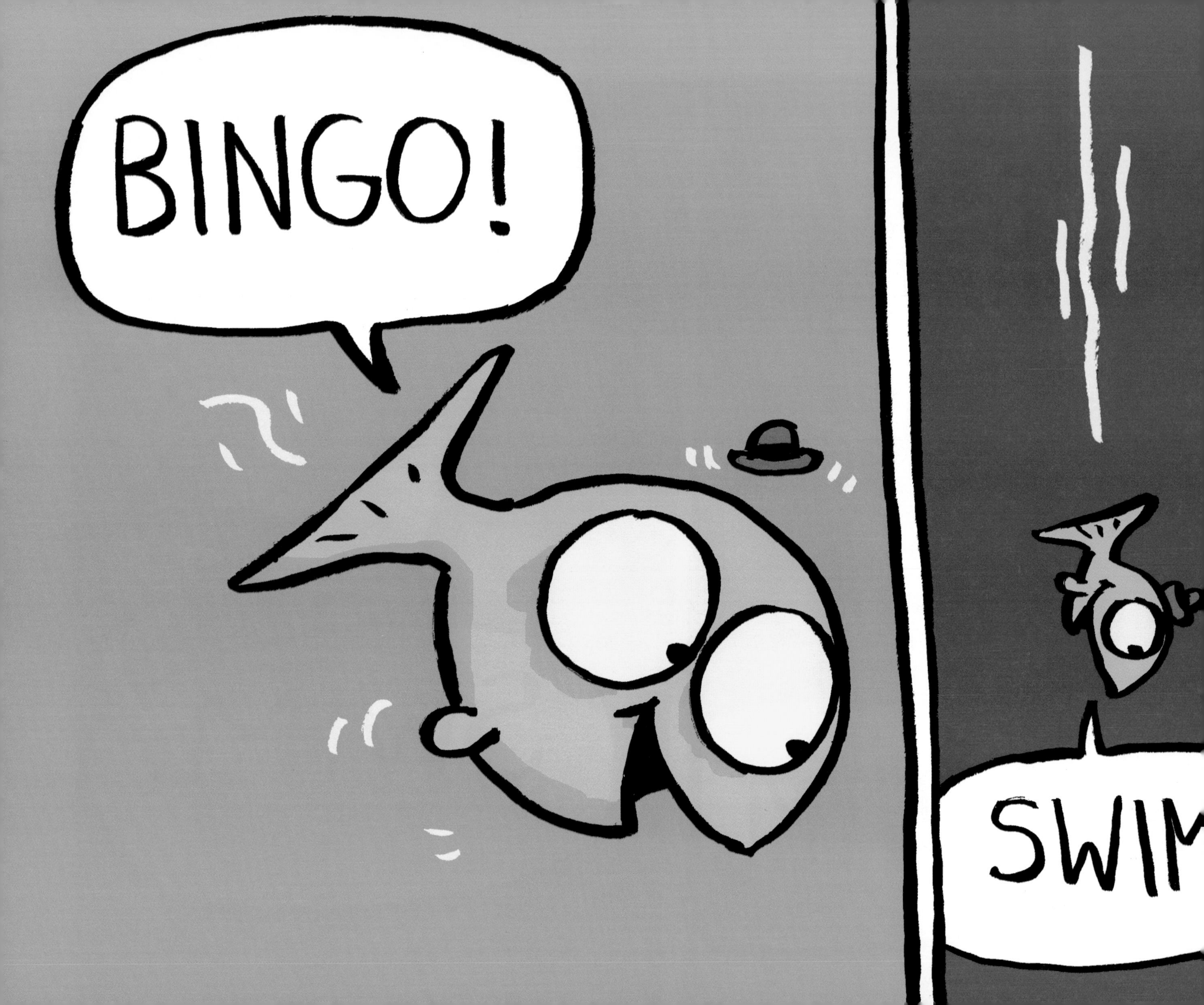
BINGO!
SWIM

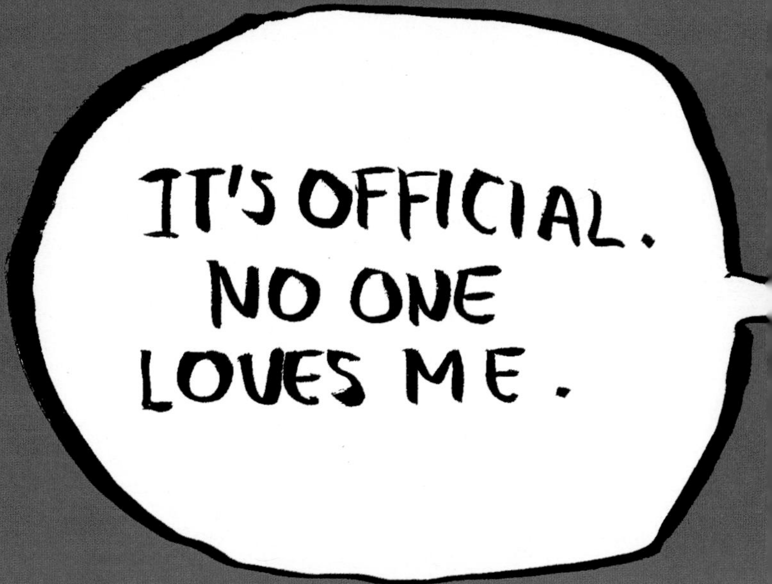
IT'S OFFICIAL. NO ONE LOVES ME.

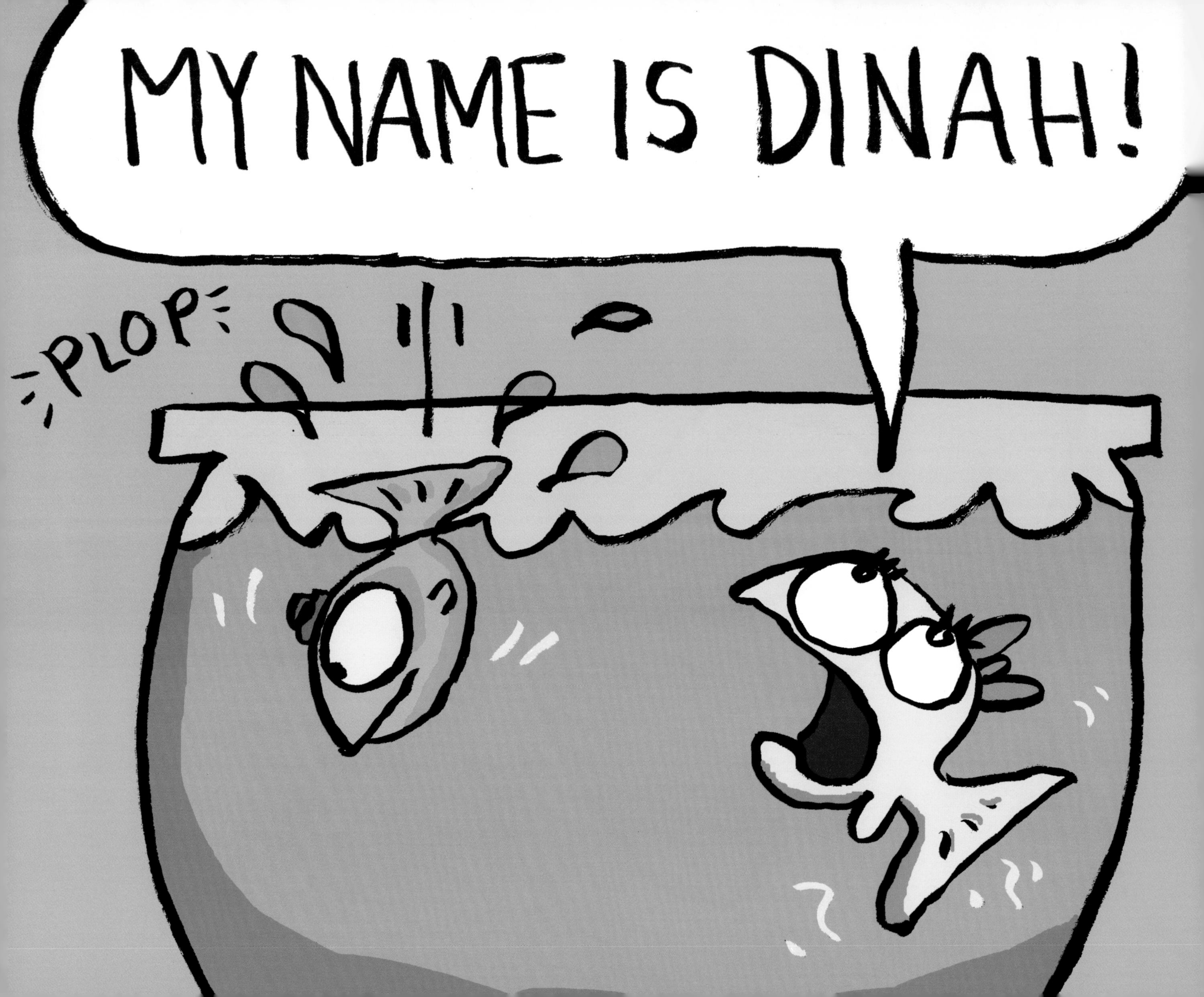
MY NAME IS DINAH!
PLOP